THE SCREECH OWL MYSTERIES

The Haunted Barn

Dedicated to
Grant Stuart Williams
and all the other Screech Owls in the world.

Produced by Salem Press, Inc.

∞ The paper used in this book conforms to the American National Standard for Permanence of Paper for Printed Library Materials, Z39.48-1984.

Library of Congress Cataloging-in-Publication Data
Garrett, Sandra G., 1950-
    The haunted barn / by Sandra G. Garrett, Philip C. Williams.
        p.   cm. — (Screech Owl mysteries)
    Summary: The Screech Owls, a group of multi-ethnic children who like to solve mysteries, combine their efforts to solve the mystery of the haunted barn.
        ISBN 0-86625-505-2
    [1. Mystery and detective stories.] I. Williams, Philip C., 1952-   . II. Title. III. Series: Garrett, Sandra G., 1950-   Screech Owl mysteries.
PZ7.G18465Hau   1994
[Fic]—dc20

93-38341
CIP
AC

First Printing

PRINTED IN THE UNITED STATES OF AMERICA

THE HAUNTED BARN

Written by

Philip C. Williams *and* **Sandra G. Garrett**

Illustrated by

Kimberly L. Dawson Kurnizki

Rourke Publications, Inc.

The moon was blood red when Jennie began her ghost story. Her fellow members of the Screech Owls club had built a campfire near the hidden lagoon. Autumn was approaching, and the night air felt chilly and crisp. A light breeze rattled the branches of the trees. The children huddled close to the fire.

Jennie told her story with her hands. She was deaf and mute, but she had taught the other club members—Derek, Mei-Li, Luis, Rebecca, and Tommy—to read sign language. They were all good at sign language, and she was good at reading their lips when they spoke aloud.

"My dad's grandfather was born in Scotland. He told this story to my dad when he was just a little boy, and Dad told it to me." Jennie's eyes glowed brightly in the golden light of the campfire as Jennie began to sign her story. "It was a bitter, cold night. Snow had fallen a foot deep, and there was ice on Loch Ness. Young Johnny McLaren bundled up warmly and grabbed his fishing pole and bucket of bait.

"'Where are you going so late?' his mother asked.

"'Fishing,' young Johnny replied.

"'You'll catch your death of cold,' said his mother.

"'Oh, Mom,' said Johnny. 'I'll be warm enough.'

"'Just you take the nice wool sweater I knitted for you and a warm coat besides,' said his mother.

"Johnny quickly put on the sweater and coat, lit his father's kerosene lantern, and hurried out to the loch."

As Rebecca listened, she gazed out at the water. She pretended that she was in Scotland on the banks of the loch. As the campfire crackled and snapped, the red glow of the harvest moon was reflected in the water. To Rebecca, the red sparkles looked like the rubies of a mermaid's necklace. She daydreamed that she was a mermaid, swimming quietly in the water, listening to Jennie's story.

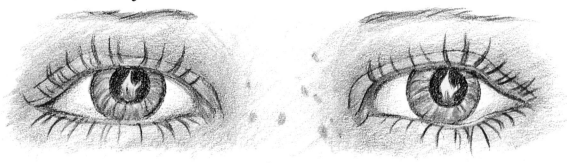

"Young Johnny walked past the ruins of an old castle," Jennie continued. "The stone walls glistened with ice and snow. When he reached the banks of Loch Ness, he fastened some bait on his hook. No sooner had he dropped his line in the water than he felt a yank that almost knocked him over.

"'Must be a big one,' he thought, and when he pulled on the line, his fishing pole broke in half."

The orange light of the campfire flickered on Jennie's face and hands as they told her story. Long shadows fell deep into the woods surrounding the lagoon.

"Suddenly," Jennie went on, clenching her fists and waving her hands in the air, "Johnny saw the green, scaly head of a dragon just a few feet from the shore. Its mouth was wide and its teeth were razor sharp."

Mei-Li could feel goose bumps on her arms. It was fun to be a little bit scared.

The children's eyes grew wide as they watched Jennie's hands. An owl hooted in the distance.

"The dragon roared and its nostrils flared wide. Johnny could see all the way down into its dark, gurgling throat.

"Johnny dropped his pole and ran as fast as he could all the way home. He told his mother and father about the dragon, but they did not seem surprised.

"'You've seen the Loch Ness monster,' his mother said. "'Aye,' his father said, 'old Nessie paid you a visit.'

"To this day, people travel from all around the world to try to see old Nessie, the Loch Ness monster." Jennie's hands fell to her lap as they ended the story.

Everyone was quiet. Finally, Mei-Li spoke.

"Wow, Jennie," she said. "That was spooky."

"Y-yeah," said Luis, looking over his shoulder. "Do you think there are any dragons out here?"

The children shuddered and stared out at the water, still reflecting the red harvest moon.

* * * * * *

"Who's next?" asked Derek.

"My turn," said Tommy. He patted his dog Wolf, who lay beside him.

"Hang on a second," Derek said. He reached down and turned on the cassette recorder in his knapsack. "Okay. You can start now." Derek was recording ghost stories for the Screech Owls's upcoming Halloween party. He liked to play with electrical gadgets, most of all his dad's computer.

The owl hooted again. Wolf raised his head from his paws and whined.

"That owl reminds me of an old Makah legend handed down by my people." Tommy began. "It was about a wise old woman who put her spirit into an owl when she died." Tommy's voice sounded eerie and low, like the owl in his story.

"The owl slept in the trees over the old woman's grave and warned children to listen to the advice of their elders," he added.

"Yet there were two children in the village—a brother and sister—who laughed at the legend and said that it wasn't true. They said the grown-ups had made it up to get the children to obey them.

"These two children ignored their parents and did pretty much what they wanted to do. They wouldn't eat their dinner. They would eat only junk food. They would run away and play instead of doing their chores."

A gust of wind stirred sparks in the campfire.

"One night they decided that they weren't going to bed, so they left the village and went into the forest. As they left, an owl flew over them and hooted. 'Go back! Go back!' it seemed to say. They just laughed and ran away.

"Suddenly a mountain lion jumped out of the bushes and stood in front of them, licking its lips. 'Don't you children know you shouldn't be out in the forest at night?' it asked. 'I always know when children disobey their elders and come out into the forest alone.' The children screamed and . . ."

Tommy stopped talking as a low, wailing sound came from a nearby pasture. Wolf growled and stood up.

"W-what was that?" Luis said. His eyes were wide.

"What did you hear?" signed Jennie.

"Something is out there," Luis signed back.

"Let's go see what it is," Tommy said, grabbing his flashlight.

The other children followed Tommy and Wolf. They walked slowly through the woods, toward the pasture.

"*Maa-a-ah!*"

"There it is again!" Rebecca said.

"Sounds like it's coming from that old barn in the pasture," Derek said. "Maybe it's a cow."

"Or a goat," said Mei-Li.

"That barn is part of the old Smith farm," Tommy said. "No one has lived there for years. We'd better go investigate."

"I don't think that's such a good idea," Luis said. "What if it's a mountain lion?"

"Or the old owl woman," Rebecca said.

"Or the Loch Ness monster," Derek said.

"Look!" Mei-Li whispered, pointing. "I saw a face peeking through the door of the barn. I think it was an owl face!"

Just then the barn door swung on its hinges and a dark shape moved toward them.

"*Maa-a-ah!*" it cried.

"Run!" yelled Luis. "It's a mountain lion!"

"No, it's a big owl!" Mei-Li screamed. She snapped a quick photograph with the camera she carries everywhere.

Wolf started toward the shape, barking fiercely.

"Come on, Wolf," Tommy yelled. "We don't know what it is!"

The children, followed by Wolf, ran back to the comforting light of the campfire. They listened carefully but did not hear the wailing sound again. Tommy shined his flashlight into the woods, but the creature did not seem to be following them. Something splashed in the water behind him. He turned his flashlight to the lagoon, but everything was still and dark. Even the harvest moon had disappeared behind a cloud.

"Let's go home," Luis said. "I don't like being stuck between a mountain lion and a sea monster." He pulled his baseball cap down lower on his head. "I wish I had my bat," he said, looking over his shoulder.

"Y-yeah," stuttered Mei-Li. "Ghost stories are fun, but not when they're real."

The others agreed. They put out the fire and walked close to Tommy's flashlight as they headed for home.

* * * * * *

16

Early the next morning, Derek called a meeting of the Screech Owls at the tool shed in his backyard. The shed was their clubhouse.

When the others arrived, Derek held up his cassette recorder. "Listen to this," he said. "I recorded those sounds we heard coming from the old barn." He turned on the recorder. "*Maa-a-ah*," the ghostly voice wailed. The children listened to the noise several times.

"It doesn't sound like any animal I've ever heard," Tommy said.

"This picture isn't much help either," Mei-Li said. She showed the others her blurry photograph of the old barn. It was impossible to tell what was coming through the door.

"I read somewhere that you can't take a picture of a ghost," Luis said. "They just show up as blurs in a photo. Like that one."

"We formed the Screech Owls club to solve mysteries," Derek said. "Looks like we've got a good one."

"We should go back to the old barn now, while it's light, and investigate," Jennie signed.

"I don't know," Luis said. "What if the ghost comes after us?"

The others were quiet. After a moment Tommy spoke. "I think we'll be okay in the daylight," he said. "Ghosts don't come out during the day, and if it's not a ghost, we've got Wolf to protect us."

"Let's vote on it," Derek said. "How many say we go?"

Six hands went up.

"It's unanimous," he said.

"Let's go!" Tommy shouted. He blew a sour note on his bugle. Wolf barked.

* * * * * *

The children hopped on their bikes and rode back to the old Smith farm.

"It doesn't seem so scary in the daytime," Rebecca said, as they approached the weather-beaten old barn. They got off their bikes and leaned them against a wooden fence.

"Let's check around outside the barn first," Tommy said.

"Derek, Jennie, and Luis, you go around that side.
Rebecca, Mei-Li, and I will look around the other side.
We'll meet at the back."

As the children circled the barn, they looked carefully
behind overgrown bushes, rusted farm machinery, and
piles of rotten lumber. Finally, the six met behind the barn.

"See anything?" Tommy asked.

"No," Derek said. "Just a lot of junk."

"Guess it's time to go inside," Tommy said. He pulled open a wooden door in the back of the barn. The door creaked loudly on rusty hinges.

The children stood just outside the door and peered in. It was dark, musty, and silent.

"Ba-a-a!"

They jumped back.

"It's in there!" Luis yelped.

The children froze, too frightened to move.

"Ba-a-a!"

"Let's go," Mei-Li said. She started to back away and the others followed. As they turned to run back to their bikes, Tommy stopped abruptly. He started to laugh.

"Look!" He pointed off to the edge of the clearing where a fat white sheep stood staring at them. "Ba-a-a," it bleated again.

"A stray sheep," Derek sighed with relief.

"Guess we solved that mystery," Jennie signed. "It must have gotten out of that pasture down the road. We should tell the owners before something happens to it." Jennie loved animals. She had two dogs, a cat, three white mice, and a hamster at home.

"Let's go home and get a snack," Luis said. "Ghost hunting makes me hungry."

They walked to their bikes and hopped on. As they started to ride away, a sound drifted out of the old barn.

"*Ma-aa-ah, Ma-aa-ah . . .*"

"There it is again!" Mei-Li exclaimed, "and that's not the sheep!"

The children stopped their bikes several feet from the front of the barn. As they stared at the door, Tommy got off his bike and bent down. He saw several small tracks in the dry soil.

"It sounds like a cat meowing," Rebecca said.

"Mountain lions are cats," Luis said nervously.

A dark shape and two eyes, about two feet off the ground, appeared in the crack of the barn door.

"I'm outta here," Luis yelled, turning his bike away from the barn.

The other children—all except Tommy—turned their bikes to follow.

"Wait," Tommy called.

They stopped and watched in amazement as Tommy and Wolf walked bravely toward the barn door. When Tommy reached the door, he pushed it open wider. A little girl, not even two years old, toddled out, crying.

"*Ma-a-ah Ma-a-ah*," she sobbed.

Wolf licked her face as Tommy tried to comfort her.

"Here's our ghost," Tommy called.

The other children gathered around. "Poor little thing," Rebecca said, wiping the little girl's face with a tissue. "Where are her parents?"

"She must be lost," Luis said. He offered the little girl a cookie from his pocket. She stopped crying and ate it hungrily.

"Let's look around," Derek said. "Maybe her mom and dad are nearby."

Five of the children searched the barn inside and out—Rebecca stayed with the baby—but there were no signs of the child's parents.

Tommy studied the ground between the barn and the woods. "Her footprints come from the woods. Let's see where they go."

Rebecca's bike had a big basket on it. They put the little girl in it and walked their bikes through the woods. Using the lessons his father had taught him about tracking, Tommy led the others to a hill.

"Seacrest State Park campground is just on the other side," Tommy said. "I don't know how she walked over that hill with those short legs, but I bet that's where she came from."

"She's a lucky little thing," Rebecca said. "That hill is loaded with poison ivy, but I don't see any bumps on her face and hands." Rebecca knew all about plants, flowers, and trees. She was always explaining them to the other Screech Owls.

"We should take her to the campground and see if her parents are looking for her," Jennie signed.

As the children approached the campground, they saw a park ranger talking with a man and woman. The woman was crying and the man looked very worried. Then the woman saw the children and screamed, "My baby! You found her!" She ran over and scooped the little girl out of the bike basket.

"Ma-Ma, Ma-Ma," said the little girl, happily.

"Where was she?" asked the park ranger.

"We found her in the barn on the other side of the woods," Tommy said.

"She must have left our tent last night after her mother and I were asleep," said the little girl's father, hugging her tightly. "We didn't even know she was gone until we woke up this morning."

"Luckily, the old barn kept her protected from the cold," Tommy said. "I'm just glad we found her."

"We want to give you a reward for bringing our little girl back," said the father.

"Oh, no," Tommy said, "my friends and I are in a club that solves mysteries. We're the Screech Owls, and we like helping people."

"The Screech Owls never accept rewards," added Luis.

"Just bringing your little girl back to you is reward enough for us," Rebecca said.

Jennie, Derek, and Mei-Li nodded their agreement.

As the Screech Owls rode away, the little girl waved. "Bye bye," she called.

They waved back and headed for home.

"You never got to finish your ghost story about the owl woman," Derek said to Tommy as they rode away.

"That's okay," Tommy laughed. "I was making it up as I went along." He blew a long, sour note on his bugle and charged ahead. The other Screech Owls laughed and followed, with Wolf howling as he ran along behind.

Glossary

campground: An area outdoors that has been set aside for living and sleeping for a short period of time.

elders: Older people. In American Indian tribes, the elders are greatly respected for their wisdom and are valued for their advice.

glimpse: A brief, quick look.

harvest moon: A full moon that is visible during the fall. Often it appears very large and orange or red in color.

investigate (in *ves* te gate): To study the facts of a situation in order to learn the truth.

Loch Ness (lock ness): A deep, narrow lake in Scotland, in the northern region of the British Isles. Many people believe that they have seen a large creature, perhaps a descendant of prehistoric times, in the lake. They have named this creature Nessie, or the Loch Ness monster.

Makah Indians (mah *kah*): An American Indian tribe that lived along the Pacific Northwest coast, near Cape Flattery in Washington State. The name Makah means "people of the cape." Today, many Makah still live on a reservation along Neah Bay, Washington, while others have moved off the reservation to live in towns and cities.

mute (mewt): Not able to speak.

poison ivy: A plant that can cause a bad rash and itching if it is touched.

reservation (rez er *vay* shen): Public land set aside for the use of American Indians.

sign language: Words formed with motions of the hands instead of sounds from the mouth. One language of hand signs is known as American Sign Language.

unanimous (yoo *nan* e mus): Agreed upon by everyone.

It makes us feel good to help people who are in distress or who cannot help themselves.